Sam Hash

Bea and the Buttersquelch

To Mandy,

Hey, here it is ...
my world of the Buttersquelch ..
Hope you find it as funny as I do.
lots of love,

europe books

\# 15

ISBN 979-12-201-0250-6
First edition: December 2020

BEA AND THE BUTTERSQUELCH

CHAPTER ONE

Bea stared at the Buttersquelch and the Buttersquelch stared right back. He stared with the complete belief that he was in fact, invisible. Telling himself that the small human stood before him was actually looking straight through him, at something clearly intriguing behind him. He was standing at the base of a ginormous Cedar tree, so perhaps this human was trying to work out a way to climb it. Though he was not sure how with those tiny hands humans have. He had almost been booted out of the way before by a massive human with massive human feet. It was kicking bits of rubbish about as it walked and he was sure he was going to be next. He remained completely frozen, not even twitching to itch his beak. Not wanting to attract any attention with movement and the human had walked straight past him.

The human that was in front of him now was much smaller, with hair. A lot more hair! It was all curly and red and sticking out in every direction. Almost like it was trying to escape from the head it was growing out of. It also had these big bizarre looking circle eyes with spikes sticking out of them. It must have bad eyes as they were held onto its head with a strap. Imagine having eyes so bad that you had to strap them onto your face to stop them falling out and rolling away! The giant human that almost kicked him before was too huge to see what sort of eyes it had. Who knows, maybe it didn't have eyes at all.

This mini human was peering round him, down to the left then down to the right. For some reason it had turned and looked behind itself and even looked up at the sky. It sniffed its nose a bit and jiggled its eyes around. (They must have come loose again.) Still, he stood unmoving, believing with complete conviction, in his invisibility.

"Why are you looking at me like that?" the mini human said looking directly at him.

The Buttersquelch humpfed a bit, let his arms hang down and fidgeted his feet. This did feel good as one of his feet was starting to get tingly. He looked up at the human, poked his bottom beak out sideways and humpfed again. He was having the realisation moment that he was not actually invisible to humans, and in fact, not invisible to anything at all. He reached the conclusion that the previous giant human had just walked past him without noticing that he was there.

"Oh well, never mind that then." He grumbled and rolled his eye.

"Never mind what?" asked the human.

"Being invisible…"

"But you're not invisible, I can see you." Stated the human as it bent down a bit to get a better look.

"Well I know that now" the Buttersquelch sputtered. He sniffed and snuffled a bit, and feeling a bit deflated he looked back up at the human with weird spikey eyes and overflowing red hair. "What are you?" Asked Bea looking down at, well, she was not sure what. This peculiar little fellow was a bit shorter than half as tall as she was with feet twice as big. He had knobbly knees and elbows attached to knobbly limbs. His head looked a bit like a squashed bird with massive ears to balance out his massive hands and feet. And although each ear was the same size as his face, it was a face that seemed to make sense. He had fur that was a glorious mix of reds and oranges and had random long feathers sticking out with purple tips topped with a twitch of blue. He was peering up at her with one massive curious eye under a rather eccentric eyebrow. The other eye was small and dark. He had a little yellow beak with the bottom half sticking out sideways, maybe because he was just not happy at the moment.

Then he stood up straight, puffed his chest out and put his bottom beak back under the top one where it belonged. Then with one outstretched finger pointing to the clouding sky he proclaimed "I am a Butter-squelch!"

"Wow...I've never met a Buttersquelch before. My name is Bea. What's yours?" Bea crouched down onto one knee so her head was almost level with his and held out her hand for a hello shake. The Buttersquelch looked quizzically at the stuck-out hand, and with the

9

eccentric eyebrow raised to an extraordinary height, put his hands on his hips and humpfed again.

"Why are you sticking your arm out at me?"

"Copy me…" said Bea, and as instructed the Buttersquelch stuck out its hand. "Now…what's your name?"

"My name is Boil." Bea took his hand in hers and shook it, almost taking him clean off his feet. He was a lot lighter than he looked like he would be, maybe his bones were part bird too thought Bea to herself.

"Hello Boil!" Bea said with a triumphant grin.

Wobbling back into balance Boil replied "Hello Bea." Boil was now clearly more relaxed and for the first time in their acquaintance they both did the same thing at the same time and smiled.

"So!" said Boil. "What sort of a human are you?"

"Well err…umm…I'm a girl. And I've just turned eight and a half."

"A girl hey…what's a girl?" asked Boil cocking his head and rocking on his heels.

"Erm…well I guess…a girl is different to a boy." Bea had never had to explain what sort of a human she was before so she wasn't exactly sure what to say.

"Oh I see." Boil peered into Beas face and pointed to the spikes with one of three long bony fingers with blue and purple fingertips. "Is that why you have those funny eyes that keep coming loose from your face? Because you are a girl…?"

"What…these?" With one hand pointed to her own face and the other resting on her belly Bea threw her head back and laughed. "Ah ha-ha-ha…no silly, these aren't my eyes. These are my goggles. They make everything look the colour of summer. Here, you try."

Bea took the goggles off her own head and leaned across to put them on her new friend. Since his ears were so massive, she pulled one through the elastic strap and sat them on his head a bit wonky over his beak. Boil pushed them on to his face making them fit better in front of his good eye. He looked up at the sky then turned to look up through the branches of the Cedar Tree. He looked at the grass, at his own feet, then spun in a circle and looked back up at Bea.

"Whoa...Wow...these are amazing. You're right! Everything looks like summer. How is this possible... some sort of magic?" Boil walked a bit as he talked, lost in the moment of something new.

"No, I wish it was magic but it's just yellow plastic. I have some purple ones at home too. Which ones I wear depends on what mood I'm in. I picked the sunny ones today as it's been raining a lot these last few days, and as much as I love watching the rain and jumping in puddles, I needed to remind myself that it's almost summer." Bea explained as she followed Boil in a big loopy ring around the base of the Cedar Tree.

After a bit more walking and talking and looking about they found a good patch of grass sprinkled with Daisies and Clover and lay down. They stuck their arms out, kicked off their shoes and looked up to the growing clouds above.

CHAPTER TWO

Bea had spent the last hour or so gazing upwards exploring the clouds that were playing overhead. The orangey hue from her goggles made them easier to watch as it softened the glare so she didn't have to squint. They were undulating, morphing, transforming from one creature to another. She chuckled to herself as the cloud formation that presently held her concentration looked like an old woman with a long witchy nose and a massive head. It had tiny arms that stuck out sideways and big kangaroo legs. As the clouds meandered across the sky it looked like the legs were walking, which escalated Bea from a giggle to a full belly laugh. Boil was dozing dreamily next to her. He had one foot twitching in conjunction with a wiggly ear, like a dog dreaming about chasing a rabbit.

"Boil..," Bea nudged Boils knobbly knee with the knobble of her own. "Boil! It's time to wake up now."

Boil rolled his head to Bea and grinned lazily. He stuck out his arms and legs as far as they would go and indulged in an extravagant yawn. He sat up with a humpf, shook bits of grass from his ears and gave his beak a good scratch.

"Yup yup yup. That was some much needed kip. Hmmm yup!" With that he stuck his arms straight up in the air, stretched out his fingers and had another, but less dramatic yawn. Then as if on cue both their bellies rumbled.

"What do you want to eat mumbly grumblyoooo…?" One belly would say to the other.

"Ooooooo, lovely munchie grumblyoooo…" the other belly would reply. "Ummm Broccoli mumbly-oooo." "Ooooo Cherry Pie umbuggly grumblyoooo." "Ummmm lovely jubbly chippies mmmm." "Oooooh yeah chippy nibbleys umbugglyoooo."

"Well Boil, by the sounds of it I think we should get some lunch. My house is behind those trees over there." Bea pointed to a path that led to a small woodland on the far side of the common. "You can hide in my gran-dads shed and I'll bring something out."

Slowly they both put their shoes on over their now slightly wet socks. This took some effort from Boil since his feet were so huge and he had to navigate his way through a bird nest of knotted laces. He had to concentrate when lifting each foot to maintain balance, this must be why he evolved with such massive hands.

"Here, you can wear these again if you want to." Bea offered Boil the goggles leaving red rings around her eyes where they had been sitting.

"That would be amazing! Yes please! These are wicked fun." Boil fixed them over one ear the same way that Bea had before and off they set to find food. Once they were on their feet the belly conversations got louder, so they both walked at a brisk pace into the trees. As the pair had almost reached the entrance to the woodland the first drops of rain began to fall.

"Here comes the rain... I wondered when it was going to get here. I was hoping we would get home first but this isn't too bad. The trees will cover us." Bea said holding both her palms up to catch raindrops.

"Humpf...speak for yourself." said Boil looking up and around. He made a clumsy dash for the trees which were just a few meters away. "I don't like getting rained on, it makes all my fur and feathers stick down." Bea had to stifle a giggle as she pictured Boil with all the fluff on his ears stuck down and his long feathers plastered to his head. Like the way a hamster looks when it is wet, all skinny with bulgy eyes. But she did not want to upset Boil further so kept this thought to herself. "Don't worry, it really isn't far, fifteen minutes at the most and we'll be there...come on." She put a comforting hand on Boils shoulder and off they went.

Bea had to admit that the path looked a lot spookier in the rain with a moody cloudy sky. They had only been walking for a few minutes before the rain had grown from a drizzle into fat raindrops, and the wind was getting livelier too. The Silver Birch and Oak Trees made a lot of noise as branches banged and switched against each other. Most of the birds, squirrels and other woodland wildlife had already hidden themselves away. The Blackberry bushes that lined either side of the path were catching their legs as they hurried past, and to make it just a little bit more challenging the path was showing the first signs of turning into mud.

"How much further is it?" Boil asked looking a bit troubled.

"Not far now, it's just round this bend. Sorry Boil, it's a nice walk when it's sunny. Are you okay?" checked Bea, concerned that her friend was having a difficult time.

"Yes, yes. Hmmmm... I'm okay. I just need to get somewhere dry. My fur keeps me warm, so when I get rained on I get extra chilly. Don't worry though, I'm alright. I'm made of tough stuff!" Boil was picking up the pace with his shoulders hunched and his head hung low, his eye focusing forwards, encouraging his body to follow.

Bea and Boil ran for the last little bit and shared a great relief when they finally reached Beas back gate. Excellently timed too as the rain was getting angrier and the wind was putting up a fight. It had taken them twenty minutes in the end, and as much as Bea loved a good variety of weather, even she would rather not be out in this. The showered pair went straight through the gate and into Beas Grandads shed.

CHAPTER THREE

As rickety as it was, it was warm and dry and almost cosy. Bea looked around for some rags to dry themselves off with. Poor Boil, what a sight. He was right, his fluffy fur had flattened to his skin and his feathers were stuck to his back and ears. The dripping from his beak began to slow along with both of their breaths. He did smell a bit odd with his wet fur, but it wasn't entirely unpleasant. It was not as bad as wet dog smell.

"You've got dirt smudges all over your cheeks now…" said Boil looking up at Bea, whilst giving his own head and arms a good shake. It did not take much before his fur was fluffy again, his feathers were back sticking up and out, and some good spirit had returned to his eye. "How do I look?" asked Boil standing proudly, grinning with both hands on his hips.

"You look wonderful Boil, truly. But I'm afraid you've got some smudges from the rags too. But better to be dry with dirty rags than to be cold and wet." The rags they used were as grubby as you would expect from something that hibernated on the floor of a very old garden shed, but could definitely have been worse.

"Here you go…" Boil was handing the goggles back

to Bea. He had slung them over his shoulder when they ran as the bouncing up and down was making them fall off his head. "I almost dropped them back there, but managed to keep them safe."

"You hang on to them a bit longer while I go and make us some food." Bea said as her belly grumbled angrily again. "I'm coming belly, I'm coming..." she said to her stomach, even looking down to face it. "Right...I'm going. Are you going to be okay waiting here?"

Boil was already looking around at all the nicks and knacks and bits and bobs. "Mmmm Hmmm. I'll be very good here, look at all these treasures you have." replied Boil, with his beak in the air absorbing his new surroundings.

"Great! I won't be long." With that Bea grabbed an old newspaper off the floor to hold over her head as she dashed up the garden path.

"Grumbly mumbly moany oh." Boils belly was trying to make conversation again. He patted his stomach telling it to wait a bit longer and he began to search the shed.

It truly was a treasure trove. There was a desk with half closed drawers overflowing with curly metal bits, shiny spikey bits and a whole rainbow of assorted electrical wires. One drawer was filled with an overwhelming amount of cloths, sponges and rags, all covered with oil patches, rust rubbings and grime. Boil especially loved the smell of the oil patches. On the desk there were all kinds of engine bits, lawnmower parts, and what looked like a dismantled radio. The kind of dismantling that would take a lifetime to put back together again.

Then, littered all over the desk, drawers and floor were a whole array of screws, nuts, bolts and nails, some old, some new, some shiny, some not. They really were scattered everywhere. Beas Grandad must have had some sort of celebration and thrown them all over himself in a fit of joy!

The other side of the shed was filled with shelves and tools hanging on hooks. There were a variety of hammers, screwdrivers, pliers and rulers. There was even an axe! Now this did grab Boils attention, so much so that it even stopped his belly rumbling. The shelves were piled high with metal objects, plastics, machines and screens. It looked like a life's work of collecting the unnecessary.

In the middle, acting as a comfy heart in the chaos of the body of the shed, was a throne of an armchair. It was a hideous green and orange, all tattered and torn. But to Boil it looked good enough for Buttersquelch royalty. His bottom beak slowly lowered and the pupil of his good eye grew large. Once he became aware of the fact that he was just standing there slack jawed he moved fluidly towards the chair. (For Boil this was no mean feat and is only achieved when he is totally captivated.) Boil was dwarfed by it, but was by no means intimidated by it and he began to climb up. As he reached the top and swung his bottom on to the cushion Bea burst through the door with some lunch.

"Whew! The rain is easing off again now. It must

have been saving itself up for us. I must say you look good up there on Grandads chair. Boil the Buttersquelch King of the shed!" This set them both off laughing and Bea almost dropped the peanut butter and blackberry jam sandwich she had just made off the plate. Grinning wildly, she went over to the armchair and passed the plate up to Boil to hold as she climbed up to join him.

"Atchew...Aaaaaatcheeeewww! Oooerr...I think the dust has set me off...Aatcheweeoo!" Poor Boil sneezed so hard that it sent him flying backwards so his feet were lifted clean into the air. "Oh, my poor brain" said Boil as he rubbed his head. "It always gets a good shake when I sneeze like that." He rubbed his beak with his arm and resumed his upright position. He looked hungrily at the deliciously wonky, extra crusty with jam overflowing sandwich on Beas lap. Bea's eyes rolled sideways along with the corner of her smile as she looked at Boil looking at the food.

"Hungry?" asked Bea.

"Oooh yeah! That Bea, is quite possibly the most beautiful sandwich I have ever seen." And with that, they picked up half a sandwich each and took gigantic mouthfuls. They would have laughed at all the jam they were splurging all over themselves but were too engrossed in satisfying the hungry rumbly bellies.

"Yup yup yup. That jam was delicious, it even had whole blackberries in it."

"Yep!" replied Bea. "My Mum makes it. We collect berries from the bushes we walked past earlier. She makes all kinds of jams, crumbles, pies and cakes. This is some of the last of the jam so I'm happy you really appreciate it. There is only one jar left now, then that's it until autumn gets here again."

"I most definitely do truly appreciate it." Boil leaned back on one elbow as the other hand rested on his now round satisfied belly.

CHAPTER FOUR

"Aha! I've had a thought!" exclaimed Boil as he sat bolt upright with one jammy finger pointed straight into the air.

"Hmmm, have a what?" asked Bea lazily as she watched the early afternoon sun making beams through the dust in the shed air.

"I have something to show you, well, to give you really. It's about time I passed it on to someone else." Boil said excitedly. Then with a calm and delicate precision he reached two of his blue fingertips into his left breast pocket. Boil had accumulated quite a collection of pockets and pouches. Some stitched, some pinned, some dangled from his belt. They were all made from a healthy mix of materials and colours and contained many different things. He even had a tiny one on the side of his right boot. He always made some sort of noise or jingle as he rattled about. He most definitely was not one of the stealthiest of Buttersquelches.

"A gift for me hey, you have my attention." This perked Bea up very quickly from her digestion rest. "What is it?"

"This," said Boil as he gently lifted a blue piece of

threadbare cloth out of his pocket and unfolded it "Is an 'I don't know what'!" It was something small with a dazzling sparkle. Boil grinned excitedly and held it in the air by a grubby piece of string that it was attached to.

"An 'I don't know what' hey, sounds interesting." The object caught a dusty sunbeam as it swung from side to side, reflecting in Beas eyes giving them an extra fiery depth. "So, what exactly is an 'I don't know what'?"

"Well err, an 'I don't know what' is an, urm, well err, well I don't muchly know." Boil replied trying desperately not to totally confuse himself. Joining in her gaze he gave it a little swing in the air, momentarily hypnotizing them both. The diffracted sun rays danced all over the shed in rainbow spots. It was actually a little chunk of Amethyst Crystal that had been dipped into something silver and tied to a bit of string.

"I found it when I was small." started Boil.

"Smaller than you are now you mean?" chuckled Bea cheekily.

"Yes Bea. Smaller than I am now." said Boil as he rolled his big eye over to her. "I found it when I was young. I've had it for so long now that I can't remember how long."

"Exactly how old are you?" asked Bea.

"Oh Bea, I'm really not too sure. I lost track some time ago. I do however, know that I am middle old." stated Boil.

"Middle old, how can something be middle old?

That doesn't make any sense." Bea screwed up her face looking a bit flummoxed.

"Well, you have young and you have old. So, I guess I am about middle old. It's quite logical when you think about it." explained Boil. "My beak is still yellow so I know I have a lot older to get. Old Buttersquelches have dark orange beaks and their ears almost touch the floor." Boil gave his own ears a rub as he imagined them being that old. "Ears never stop growing you know, so eventually they get a bit heavy to stick out sideways so they hang down. Nothing can beat gravity I guess."

"Oh." said Bea, "that does make sense. Do you get any taller?"

"Nope, this is it. I just change colour, get massive ears and might start talking gibberish from time to time, but I don't get any bigger." Boil sniffed a bit and scratched his beak as he mulled this thought over. He then looked back at his gift for Bea as it dangled from its mangled string.

"It's strange, that such a dirty bit of string can be a part of something so beautiful." remarked Bea. "I guess it's the same for most things though, we all have our scruffy bits."

"That's very insightful of you Bea, a very middle old thing to say." complimented Boil.

"Thank you Boil. I'll treasure it. It will be my new good luck charm." But before Boil could drop it into her almost outstretched hand, she pulled it back, looked straight at Boil and had her own 'Oh!' moment. "Ooooh!" shouted Bea, clearly just remembering something important. "We should put our goggles back on, I keep a spare pair in the drawers down there. Here." Bea picked up the orange goggles that were hiding behind Boil and dropped them into his lap. She hopped off the armchair and in three big strides she was at the other side of the shed. She pulled out the drawer filled with rags and sponges and reached her hand right to the back. With skilful dexterity Bea pulled out her other purple goggles. "Aha! Bingo!" Then with one swift motion Bea pulled the goggles over her head, took two big leaps back to the armchair and jumped on.

It was unfortunate that Bea jumped on at the exact moment that Boil was putting on his goggles, and in a bit of a kerfuffle, the crystal dropped itself down the crack at the back of the chair.

"Noooo." cried Bea and Boil as they watched it, in slow motion, disappear, taking with it both of their smiles. Boil heroically threw himself after it and reached his arm in as far as it would go, with his poor little beak smushed against the back of the chair.

"Urmpf, I dunno Bea...Uuurrmpf...I can't quite reach it, I have to go further!" The chair muffled Boils voice quite significantly, (as you would expect from a beak full of dusty old furniture) but Bea understood him perfectly.

"Hang on Boil...I'll hold you..." Bea shouted back. She squatted behind him and took a firm grip on both his ankles. "GO FOR IT, I'VE GOT YOU, REACH FURTHER!"

Boils entire head was now lost to a sea of green and

orange (all shades of purple now for Bea) and she was frustratingly struggling to keep hold. Then all of a sudden, whoosh! They were both sucked into the chair, like a spider that got sucked up the hoover accidentally for being in the wrong place. They were only being whooshed for a moment, but in that fraction of time Bea saw a blur of bits and bobs that her Grandad said fairies had moved over the years. On her return she would tell him that they were actually all just lost down the back of his chair.

Then Whumpf! Bea landed in a heap on Boil.

CHAPTER FIVE

"Oompf…Humpf…Ooerr…" Boil made all sorts of sounds as he got back on to his feet.

"Oh! What the, where are we, how?" Bea sputtered as she too got to her feet and dusted herself off.

"Oh bumblefluff Bea. You failed to mention that your Grandad's armchair was a portal to other worlds." Boil said this very matter of factly, like it was very common knowledge that these things even existed.

"My Grandad's armchair is a what now? Are you feeling okay Boil, did you perhaps bang your head a little too hard back there?" Bea asked with a genuine concern and looked around Boils head for lumps or bumps.

"Bea, you joke, of course you know that the chair is a portal." Boil smiled and waved his hands about. "That explains why it looks so old! It's even older than I am!"

"No Boil. I don't know what a portal is. I would have told you." Bea said looking glumly at her feet.

"Oh well, chin up kiddo. It's okay not to know things, or how would we ever learn anything?!" Boil went and stood next to her and patted her dangling deflated hand, if he could have reached her head, he would have patted that. They shared a look of acknowledgement that this was a fair enough thing to say. Bea seeing a purple Boil, and Boil seeing an orange Bea.

"Have a look around, explore a bit. You just need to acclimatize for a moment." suggested Boil.

"I guess you're right. Okay brain, calm down and engage!" Bea said this out loud to herself as she stretched her goggles to the top of her head. Boil smiled as he watched her. Bea's pupils enlarged as the world around her seemed to shrink. The wall was smooth and curved like a cave. The air was cool but not cold and was thick with an earthy aroma.

"Are we underground?" asked Bea. "It feels like we are in some sort of den." Bea was looking over past Boils head with a look of concentration furrowing her eyebrows.

"Ha-ha, almost Bea." Boil chuckled as he looked up into her face, while at the same time pointing to a Boil sized hole behind him. "If you crawl through there it takes you deep underground." Then he pointed past Bea to another Boil sized hole behind her. "If you go through that hole it takes you outside."

Bea looked over her shoulder, and then with her own humpf, she looked back down at Boil. "I think outside." assertively decided Bea. "I think we could both do with some fresh air."

Boil was happy with Beas rational thinking. It was as if she had, for a moment, forgotten that she had just been propelled into a new dimension. He was also keen to show her his world, if she liked making pictures out of clouds in her world, then she was going to love this one. As if on cue Bea asked, "How do we get back home?" as she walked to the entrance of the exit.

"Oh. Hmmm… Humpf." Boil scratched under his beak that had stuck out sideways again. That must be his thinking face thought Bea. "Well err…We have to jump, through there." he said as he gestured with his head to the direction of a muddy puddle next to the hole that led underground.

"Down where? All I see is a puddle on the floor. Am I missing something?" speculated Bea.

"Ha-ha hum, erm yes. Yes, it is the puddle. I know it's not the best position, it shouldn't be so close to the hole for downstairs. One jump into a world you know, one jump to a world you don't! But yes, you just jump in then off you go." shrugged Boil as he smirked and raised his eyebrow. "Also, there is no guarantee that you will fall back out of the portal you fell in. They all sort of join up in a portal roundabout, so it might take a few tries to get right. This particular cave will definitely take you to your world, just a few different places in your world, the next cave along has portals to a different world." tried to explain Boil.

"I think I get it." Beas face relaxed from a concentrated expression to a smile and a nose wrinkle. "It's okay Boil. We'll be fine. Let's go outside now and air our brains out."

Boil strolled out the tunnel but Bea had to crawl. Over the years Bea had crawled through some pretty disgusting things so this was easy.

"Come, come. How are you getting on back there?" checked Boil.

"I'm good thanks." replied Bea. "Almost there!" And with that Bea crawled into a warm orange light on a thick carpet of grass.

"I'm afraid these tunnels were built for Buttersquelches. Well, us and Inklebinks. But they are less than half as tall as I am and don't come inside much anyway. They seem to be happier sleeping on the backs of the Megabinks than inside." By the time Boil had finished talking Bea was standing back on her feet next to him.

They both stretched their arms up and took in big gulps of fresh air. With a good blast of oxygen to revive him Boil got very excited and started to run around in random circles making happy chattering sounds. The light was soft on Beas face, coming from two Suns that hung huge, red and low. Spaced apart like two sleepy eyes on the horizon. Bea turned to see where she had just emerged from and saw that it was the base of a tree, the biggest oldest tree that she had ever seen. It was at least fifty times the size of the Cedar Tree back home. A big ring ran all around the bottom of the trunk like a donut, with different sized holes going into it, each nicely spaced apart. It looked like it was made of mud, but very nice high quality mud, with no lumps!

CHAPTER SIX

"What was that last thing you said, something Binks? What is Binks?" Bea asked. As she said this, she noticed what looked like bits of heads and hands popping up and down and scattered all around in the grass.

"That," pointed Boil to one of the pop-corning fellows, "Is an Inklebink. And that," he said pointing to something much larger in the distance, "Is a Megabink."

"Oh, I see. Are they friendly?" queried Bea looking a touch bemused.

"Yup yup, very friendly, here come some now. Just be yourself Bea." Boil chuckled and congratulated himself on some humorous wordplay. "Be yourself Bea, Excellent."

Bea squatted down to meet the Inklebinks that were headed her way. They all looked in proportion, just really small. (really small being about fifteen centimetres.) As they got closer, there must have been about ten of them, Bea could see that they each had four arms. Instead of running they were hopping and jumping whilst frantically waving their arms all about, it looked like trying to fly in a clumsy yet explosive kind of way.

"Oooo…" "Wait…" "Yupyupyup…" "Weeee…" A

whole chorus of excited blips and squeaks gave announcement to the arrival of the Inklebinks. It turns out that six of them had come over to say hello. There were more in the distance clearly having a whale of a time jumping about and keeping the Megabinks company.

"Hello." "Hello." "Woooo." "Yupyup." they all said together whilst gathering around Beas knobbly knees, all looking up at her with shiny excited eyes, all of their arms jittering. These little fellows were brimming with energy and Bea got a really happy feeling from them.

Boil sat next to her on the floor with his feet stuck out in front of him and he was having an animated conversation with two of them. They were clearly old friends, all pointing and waving as they shared stories.

"Hello to all of you too," Bea said looking around. "My name is Bea. It's a pleasure to meet all of you."

"Hullo." "Squeak." "Yup." "Hieee." they all sputtered together. Some of them were patting Beas knee where they could reach it. Bea held out her hand to touch one of them, and they reciprocated by rubbing his face on her finger. She replied with a little wiggle back. They all laughed at this with great delight.

"Boil, this is great! What happy little people." Bea shifted onto her other knee and looked over to him.

"Yup yup. It's hard to feel any kind of bad in their company. They truly are the happiest people you will ever meet. They don't have much in the way of vocabulary though. They mostly pick up on your energy vibrations." described Boil.

"Energy vibrations? What do you mean, that they can

tell how I'm feeling?" Bea looked about smiling and summoned all the positive energy she could.

"Sort of," replied Boil. "They can tell if you are good or if you are not. If not then they stay hidden in the grass and ignore you. If you are, they'll come and jump all over you and treat you like one of their own."

"Food." "Eeak." "Munch." "Yupyupyup." They patted Beas knee again to get her attention and pointed over to the grass with the rest of their hands.

"Hmmm. Excellent, they are inviting us to dinner." said Boil as he winked his eye at his two friends and stood up with a creaky humpf. "Let's go, I can always eat. These Binks can really cook too. A happy chef makes all the difference." As Boil licked his beak he scratched his ears and followed the Inklebinks through the grass.

"Sounds great," Bea said as she followed too. They arrived at a clearing with a big pot in the centre. Well, perhaps more of a giant frying pan than a pot, which was sizzling over smoky embers. Two of the Binks were stirring chunks of some kind of bright purple vegetable in spices. Bea had no idea what it was but it smelled divine. Other Binks skipped and ran around the pan chucking in more lovely chunks.

"Aaaah." said Boil sniffing the air, dancing his fingers about wafting more of the smell to his face. "I see snap roots are in season." He picked up two sticks from the pile next to the pot and handed one to Bea. The aroma had also caught the attention of one of the Megabinks which had started to make its way over. Now these were strange looking beasts.

"Boil," Bea tapped one of Boils ears. She was aiming for his shoulder but with her eyes fixed on what was approaching, she missed. "Boil," she tapped again.

"What's up kiddo?" asked Boil keeping his eye on the food but pricking his ears.

"Are those friendly too?" asked Bea. She was curious but not afraid. She figured they must have a docile temperament to spend their time surrounded by these crazy little Inklebinks.

"What was that?" Boil now tore his eyes away from the pot and looked at the massive eyeball on legs slowly bobbing its way towards them. "Oh yes, I know the Megabinks look nothing like the Inklebinks but they are fairly friendly. Think of them like you would a massive cow. They can't talk though. They'll just stare at you for a while then wonder off. You can ride them though, they're used to it." Boil looked like he was remembering his own interactions with them. "The Binks get up there five or six at a time to sleep. I guess it's safer up there than on the ground. Warmer too! They have really thick fur." Then Boil looked back at the food and salivated with the sizzle.

CHAPTER SEVEN

"You have time for a ride but you will have to go now, they go to sleep when the sun goes down so they are getting a smidge sleepy," recommended Boil. Bea looked down at him a bit unsure of herself. "It's fine, trust me. I do it all the time."

"How do I get on?" asked Bea as she looked at the Megabink in front of her, rolling its inquisitive eye over the landscape.

"Ah, stand up to get attention. Then when it looks at you, just look back and smile while holding your hands in the air. That way it knows you want to go up. Then climb up behind one of its ears," said Boil as he pointed to its giant ears that framed its immense eye. "I'll save you some snap root." Boil was grinning even more insanely than when he was given his goggles and was evidently blissfully happy.

"Okay, if you say so. I trust you." Bea stood still and waited for the Megabink to get closer and notice her. It was so large that once directly in front of her Bea could feel its body heat. It must have been the size of three elephants! It must look the size of the sky to the Inklebinks. 'Okay Bea' she told herself. 'Brain of a cow, brain of a cow, brain of a cow,' she repeated the cow mantra to herself as a way to keep calm. She did feel more at ease but couldn't help feeling a bit apprehensive. The creature moved slowly and seemed kind enough, it just looked so weird!

Where its face would usually sit, was one enormous eyeball, that was peering down examining the human being presenting herself. This one had an orange eye, a colour almost as deep as the suns, framed by two fluffy ears that stuck out sideways like Boils. It was a bit hunched over, the way an animal would if it walked on four legs, but this just walked on its back two. It had two huge wide back legs that walked on squishy foot pads. It had two long slender arms with hands that looked more like a bird wing with thumbs. This magical animal had a deep blue fluffy fur on its ears that faded to a lighter blue as it cascaded over its body, with a big white patch on its belly.

It stopped right in front of Bea and sat back on its haunches. When it leaned down Bea could see her reflection in its never-ending pupil, an eye so large and calm that it instantly got rid of any doubts that Bea had left.

"Urm, hi" Bea said. Then, as instructed, she held up both arms over her head and into the air. The eye rolled up a bit as if looking at something over Beas head, then tilted sideways so one of its ears brushed against the grass at her feet. Bea walked behind its ear keeping her hand on it as she moved. Its fur was so soft and Bea had never felt anything like it. She leaned inwards and brushed her check on it, eyes closed with a dreamy grin.

Now stood at the nook at the back of its ear, Bea

rubbed her other hand along its neck the same way that you would stroke a horse. This was just a monumental fluffy horse cow.

Bea jumped up as she pushed down on the Megabinks ear with her left hand while throwing her right arm and leg over its neck. She didn't quite make it all of the way and landed a bit squiffy. The gentle beast shook its head and neck a bit and shimmied her over to the middle, she barley fit over its neck and both her feet stuck out sideways. But the fur was so thick and deep that she was snug and extremely comfy. When she leaned forwards she could just about reach where its ears joined on to its head and her face smushed into its endless blue fur.

Bea sat up again and looked behind her. Along its back were small round patches of squashed down fur, this must be where the Inklebinks curl up to sleep. The thought of it made her own eyes heavy and she gave a thoughtful sigh.

With eyes front and a good grip with both hands the Megabink elevated its head and pushed itself up from its seated position. It was a smooth journey upwards, much nicer than being spat out the back of an armchair. It felt almost as if it was on rollers instead of feet, a gentle rocking from side to side, it was relaxing and soothing. Bea expected it to be a lot more jumpy but guessed its elephantine back legs acted as shock absorbers, like giant sponges to suck up the bumps.

Bea was not entirely sure how much time had passed, it all seemed so irrelevant here, but it had gotten a smudge darker. The Suns were just poking over the grass and instinctively the Megabink turned to head back to the cooking pot. Bea laughed at the sight of Boil sat with the Inklebinks eating the snap roots off the sticks. Both of his ears were jiggling as he was eating and making happy chirpy noises at the same time.

The Megabink lowered its head to the grass and gave its neck a shimmy wiggle to help Bea slide off.

"Thank you" said Bea. "That was like the very best hug I ever had. Bea nuzzled its ear with her face a final time as she let go. Then it stood up, strode off a short way and walked in a circle to flatten down some grass, then laid itself down to sleep. It did the same thing that a cat does when preparing itself for a nap, but is much less fussy.

Bea dropped on the floor next to Boil, crossed her legs, and laid back. "That was incredible." said Bea dreamily, closing her eyes and hanging on to the warm feeling, burning it into her memory. Forcing the smell, the touch on her cheeks and the vibrant blue fur into a memory she can always fall back on. She let her mind fall into the rhythm of the Megabinks walk, indulging in it.

After a few minutes she sat back up and shook the grass out of her hair. She did not do a very good job though as there was still half a garden left up there. She looked over at Boil who had two sticks of snap root waiting for her.

CHAPTER EIGHT

"Here you go, eat up." Boil passed the two snap root kebabs to Bea and nudged a dipping bowl with the tip of his toe. "This is a very delectable grass sauce to dip it in. I tell you, these little chaps make this grass taste better than I ever could." Bea dunked the snap root in the grass sauce and nodded to Boil in agreement as she had a satisfying munch.

"I knew you would enjoy a Megabink ride. I remember when I had a go as a young Buttersquelch, I refused to come off! I waited until it lay down to go to sleep, and even then, it had to give me a good shake. Aaahhh, happy times" reminisced Boil. "I still love it. There truly is nothing else in this world like it, probably nothing in any of our worlds as comfy as that." Boil looked over at Bea with a smile full of memory as she finished the last mouthful of snap.

"Thank you very much, all of you." Bea held up her two empty kebab sticks and bowed her head in appreciation to the collection of Inklebink chefs, and to the now small crowd of others who had gathered to look at the human. Full bellies seemed to slow them down. Now most were sat or laying down twiddling tufts of grass with their multitude of fingers. They all chattered and clicked and bobbed their heads bout, it was like watching a sea of jelly that kept wobbling. Bea imagined them wobbling their sleep as they dreamed about things which made her laugh to herself.

A couple of the Inklebinks were particularly curious. Two of them stood right in front of Bea and looked up onto her face with stretched toothy grins, glistening starry eyes and arms reaching up to the sky. Bea, (now understanding the signal) lowered both her arms so they had one each to climb on. It was a strange sensation, having a very mini person with four arms climbing up you, and Bea giggled as it tickled.

"Okay," said Bea looking from one to the other. "You can only play up here for a bit as we need to get moving soon." Bea knew they could not really understand what she was saying, but they interpreted the tone of her voice and emotional vibrations and both nodded their heads.

The one on her left sat on her knee while the other scampered up her right arm to her shoulder. Then stood up, hanging onto her ear for balance and reached up high to touch one of the spikes of the goggles that were resting on her head.

"Oh, I'd forgotten they were up there." Bea instinctively patted her hand on her head the same way her Grandad does when checking his head for lost specs, which was generally most of the time. "I must look bizarre from down there with these on my head, here you go," Bea lifted the goggles from her head and gave it a scratch, then dropped the goggles into her lap for the Binks to get a better look. The one on her shoulder jumped down with a nimble bounce vocalising a musical array of 'Ooooos', and 'Wooooooos'.

"How are you getting on with yours?" Bea asked Boil.

"Good. They are getting a bit itchy on my eyebrow but are comfy enough. I think my ears hold them up well." Boil rubbed both of his ears affectionately like he was thanking them for doing a good job. Then lifted his goggles and put them on the ground for the growing number of admiring staring Inklebink to play with. They made all sorts of giggly squeaky sounds and laughs. Bending over to look through and making their home turn to shades of yellow or purple. The two on Beas lap must have been especially captivated as they both went quiet and fairly still.

One of the Binks that approached Boils goggles bust have accumulated quite a static charge through the day because as he poked out his finger to touch the tip of one of the spikes he flew right up into the air from a static electric shock! He really did go flying, making a 'Weeee' sound as he went. When he landed all of his hair was stuck out sideways including the bushy hair that stuck out of his ears. The little fellow did look funny, looking about and gathering himself whilst blinking quite a lot.

"Oooo, eeerky, yipes!" and with that he gave his head a good shake like a dog shaking off a puddle that it had just destroyed, and fearlessly ran straight back over.

This time though he gingerly poked it. Then, with no reaction, he rubbed his hands all over it, followed by his face. This made his fellow Binks howl with laughter and they all squished their faces over the lenses.

Whilst their hosts were entertaining themselves Bea and Boil leant back on their elbows with a sigh.

"We need to think about moving on" said Bea. "The Suns are almost completely down and I've no idea what time it is back home."

"Nup nup nup. It won't be tomorrow there yet. Days and nights happen a lot faster here, the time will not have moved very far at your house." Boil wrinkled his face and scratched a bit and slowly made his way to his feet. "Sorry fella's, I need these back now." Boil bent down to retrieve his goggles and put them back on his head.

As Bea lifted her goggles up one of the Inklebinks climbed down from knee to foot to grass. Bea held the goggles right out in front of her as she stood up, but the remaining Bink was still hanging on tight, feet dangling and still smiling. She had a superhuman grip for such tiny hands, just like a new born baby.

"Tinks, Tinks" the Inklebink pipped. "Tinks come, cha cha ha-ha-ha…" With two hands clutching on she pointed up at Bea with her third and to herself with the fourth. Her legs danced and dangled on an invisible floor.

"Oh, I don't know, you'll have to ask Boil really. I don't know what I'm doing or where I'm going." Bea used one hand to support Tinks feet and they both looked sideways to Boil.

"Humpf! I really don't know at all." Boil paced in a circle a bit with one hand on his hip and the other scratching his bottom beak. He was watching his own feet as he contemplated.

"I think she should come with us Boil. At least you know there is a portal at my house so you can both get back. Believe me, that armchair is not going any-where." Bea lifted her hand so Tinks could step across onto her shoulder, then set her own goggles over her rather grass filled head and fidgeted them into place. Tinks sat with her legs dangling forwards, two hands patting each knee, one hand holding the elastic strap over Beas ear with the fourth waving at the crowd of Inklebinks below.

At the moment Boils vibrations were all up, down and sideways. It was too confusing for Tinks to tell what Boil was feeling as he was still making up his mind. Buttersquelches were always a bit more effort to read as they were generally a bit frantic and inde-cisive.

Boil was thinking about being responsible in case something went wrong or they got utterly lost. Boil had only ever had to look after himself up to this point, he had been on his own for so long he had gotten used to it. However, he was enjoying Beas company, and she did have a point in that they could easily get home again once they had got Bea back.

Tinks smiled more now and closed her eyes; she could feel that Boil had made up his mind. He was now releasing steady vibrations with a calm pulse. "Yup yup

yup" said Tinks to herself. This was good. This was exactly the place she was supposed to be right now.

"Hmmm, okay then." Boil finally said out loud.

"Yay! Oh Boil, you won't regret it." Beas excitement was evident. She joined all the other Inklebinks (who had all known what decision Boil would make before he even knew it himself), who were jumping, pogoing and running in zig zags with their arms in the air all laughing and chattering. Bea held her arms in the air too and spun around, but not too much, as she did not want to send Tinks flying off her shoulder.

"Come on then, let's head back to the tree. Say you're goodbye's." said Boil.

"Byeeee, bye." waved Bea as she looked across to her new friends. The Megabink she had been riding was fast asleep. She could see steam plumes rising from its, err...well she was not sure where it breathed from but it was clearly breathing from somewhere.

"Bye...Eeeek...Byebinks..." chorused a mass of heads and hands all exploding from the grass.

"Bye for now, thanks again for the food..." waved Boil as he turned and walked away with Bea falling in step behind him.

CHAPTER NINE

The tree looked truly ancient saturated in the sunset light. The deep pinks and oranges made the centuries old grooves in the bark look as deep as canyons, each one a potential for a whole new world. Perhaps they were! Who knows? Insects must need portals too. Speaking of which, the dusk brought with it a whole cacophony of bugs, critters and night life. Some flew about making darts of light through the air as their abdomens glowed. Bea could hear more than she could see, although she could see some. All sorts of insects, birds and animals that came awake at night had begun their conversations.

As they reached the base of the tree and Bea focused her attention, she could see what looked like caterpillars crawling up and in the bark. They were the same colour as the tree so she only spotted them when they moved.

"Ah, Snubgrub, tasty," Boil leaned right across Bea and picked up the bug with his beak. He tossed it into the air, caught it with his open beak and gulped it down. "Mmmm, love a Snubgrub!" declared Boil as he licked his beak.

"Boil, why did you do that?" asked Bea a bit taken aback.

"Well, coz it was there. I am part bird you know, I enjoy eating bugs. They taste nice." replied Boil, a bit surprised that he had to justify his foodie favourites. "I don't usually spot them as they only come out in the dark, and as you saw they are very well camouflaged. It's because you have two good eyes, you can see much better than me."

"I guess so. Well, if I spot anymore, I'll be sure to let you know." Bea thought that was fair enough. "Do you eat grubs Tinks?" Bea looked to her shoulder but Tinks just shrugged with two arms and pointed to the sky with a third. "Yeah, you're right. We need to get into the tree now. It really has gotten dark quickly. Bea stopped short as they reached the Buttersquelch sized tunnel and saw several more tunnels the same size going round the base of the tree. "Boil,"

"Yes Bea" answered Boil.

"How do we know this is the tunnel we came out of, they all look the same apart from the massive ones, this isn't the only hole your size?"

"Hmmmm!" Boil humpfed with both hands on his hips and looked up and down. "I think this is the right one, we'll just have to give it a go, it's definitely one of these. Besides the portal puddle being next to the burrow in the exact same place in every cave, every cave also looks the same. The only way to tell any difference is by the size of the entrance tunnel." Boil pointed to the enormous Megabink hole to the left. "I mean imagine a Megabink trying to squeeze through this tiny hole." Boil did have a chuckle at the thought of this. "At least we have this one as a starting point, then we can work our way round to the right. If we land somewhere unknown, we just have to turn around and jump straight back. But please, make sure you don't wonder off or you might lose where you landed."

Boil was clearly talking from experience.

"Okay, I trust you, let's head in." Bea lifted Tinks down then got on all fours to crawl through. Boil strolled, Tinks hopped and Bea crawled. They spilled out into the cave which did indeed have another Buttersquelch sized hole opposite accompanied by a muddy looking puddle.

"Come on, don't overthink it. Just jump straight in like me." Boil ran over to the puddle in a few wonky leaps, jumped up, pulled his feet together and his arms in tight and went feet first through the puddle. Bea was expecting a splash, (as one would) but this made a bit of a wobble sound and that was it. Even Tinks looked a bit underwhelmed and she got excited at everything. Bea also imagined that being a portal to another world it would be a bit more dramatic, at least some light flashes or something theatrical, but evidently this was not to be. This was a plain puddle that made no splash.

"Well, our turn now Tinks, you copy what Boil did then I'll go..." said Bea. But Tinks, understanding very little of this (or perhaps just not caring) ran at it like something possessed with arms and legs sticking right out and bombed in with an ecstatic 'Eeeeek', making a barely noticeable wibble as she went through. Bea did exactly the same as Boil but pulled her goggles into place first. Then within the blink of an eye she had jumped, and landed once again, in a pile on Boil.

"Oops, sorry mate, I'll go first next time hey" joked Bea with a slightly embarrassed blush. She did not want to keep squishing Boil, it just seemed to keep on happening.

Upon landing it was not entirely obvious that they were not back in Bea's shed. It was dark and cool so it took a moment for their eyes to adjust. It was quiet and there was a presence of something alive all around them. Literally! The floor and walls seemed to be aware of them.

The floor was like a really lush deep pile carpet, but it moved! It was like peering into a magic eye picture, like when you see something move out the corner of your eye but it changes when you look directly at it. It was hypnotic.

"Don't move anybody, don't wonder off or you might not find your way back" advised a concerned looking Boil. He held his arms out sideways to stop Bea moving forwards.

"Don't think we have a problem there Boil, look down at your feet." said a grinning Bea who then looked back down at her own. Boil followed her line of sight and looked down.

"Whoa! Would you look at that! It would appear that the floor likes us, ha-ha-ha." clucked Boil. What looked like thick carpet threads, were actually some sort of mushrooms. Some were stringy, some squelchy, some long, some small, but all of the fungi were moving slowly. The caps opened and tendrils wrapped themselves around their shoes, climbing completely over Tinks. She barely had two arms and one eye showing but managed to shove them off and climb to Beas knee for refuge. This was the perfect observational spot. From here she could still look down and see the sea of mushrooms unfurling and coming alive below.

The caps were all the shades of blue and purple that you could imagine, from deep indigos to shimmering ultra-marines and some like a true-blue sky. They grew up and around each other with glowing green and yellow stalks. As the caps opened, they released spores, filling the whole lower half of the space with a fine mist. It only reached as high as Beas face but totally enveloped Boil and Tinks.

It was impossible to look away and seemed to put them all in some sort of trance. It was overwhelming, but okay. Like the way it feels just before you fall asleep when your body is heavy but your brain is still slowing down and is still a bit aware of what is going on. Just as Bea was thinking this Boil got too sleepy and actually fell forwards, right onto his face. It did not hurt him as the floor was squishy mushrooms but the shock of it woke him with a start.

"Oh, hey, where am I?" said a confused looking Boil. As he started to talk the mist began to clear and his memory kicked in. Bea looked dreamy but awake, but Tinks had somehow managed to fall asleep while remaining attached to Beas knee, she was even snoring a bit too. Inklebinks truly did have an impressive grip.

Boil slowly slid his feet out of the nest of mushrooms that had built around them and gave Beas hand a wiggle.

"Bea, Bea, you with us? I think we were almost dinner there." Boil turned the gentle shake into a vigorous arm wobble and Bea came back to life. She had a yawn, lifted her goggles on top of her head and gave her eyes a tired rub.

"Hey Boil, where are we again?" asked Bea looking around waiting for her memory to also swing back into action. "I feel like I've been asleep, how long do you think we have been here?"

"I don't think very long, but we need to turn around and jump back out. I do know that we did not walk about anywhere." Boil turned and began to feel along the wall behind him.

The walls and ceiling were as equally alive as the floor. Every space was crammed with corals and sponges and full of tiny holes, like a whole coral reef without the ocean. Crawling in and around these teeny holes were spaghetti like worms. They all seemed to get exponentially larger the moment they came out of hiding. When they stretched right out, they opened their eyes, all of them! These were very bizarre indeed.

"Boil, have you seen this, these worms have twenty eyes each!" Bea stared at the wall which was fast becoming another weirdest thing she had ever seen. It sucked in all of her attention and she was lost to this growing wall of worms with complete fascination.

"Wow, well there's something you don't see every

day eh!" observed Boil. The worms had eyes that were all clustered and bunched together on its apparent head. Some were all clumped together like a bunch of grapes whilst other eyeballs were stuck out a bit like a snails. All together they looked like weird shiny dandelion flowers, ready to be blown into the wind as they blinked.

The bodies of these worms were all shades of cherry reds, sunrise pinks and floral oranges. The colour was moving up and down their bodies like a cuttlefish. It was strange to watch something with so much movement be so silent. It felt like the energy of this new place was being transmitted directly into your brain.

"Okay then Boil. We just turn around and jump straight back through yes?" Bea did an about turn of 180 degrees and felt Tinks nuzzle against her knee. "Oops, forgot she was there" Bea admitted as she looked down.

"I'll get her" said Boil as he leaned across and slowly uncurled Tinks limbs. He carried her in one hand as he patted along the wall with his other.

"Sorry about that. ooooer, sorry again," Boil was trying to be careful but he couldn't help poking a few of the worms in their many eyes.

As if picking up on what needed to be done (and not wanting to keep being poked in the eye) all of the worms turned their heads in towards one point in the wall. It was about a foot off the floor and was the same texture as the coral but was flattened down. Boil would have found it eventually but was grateful for the help.

"You hang on to Tinks and I'll go first." Bea squatted down and decided to go head first. She got her head and shoulders in and the portal did the rest. In a fraction of a moment Bea was spat out on the now familiar floor of the cave of Boils world. Before she had time to stand and turn Boil and Tinks were spat out too. Tinks was awake and on her feet, and poor Boil looked as if he had spent the day bouncing around an interesting mix of dimensions.

"How are you feeling Boil?" asked Bea putting a hand on his shoulder.

"Aaaah, hmmmm, yup. I'm good, shall we try next door?" Boil said as he yawned and headed towards the outside hole.

CHAPTER TEN

Bea, Boil and Tinks turned left out the cave to the next cave along, which they entered in the prescribed order of Boil strolling, Tinks bouncing and Bea crawling.

"Blimey Boil, all of this portal jumping certainly keeps you fit. I feel like I've completed my school's cross country track in record time." puffed out Bea.

"Yup yup yup." Boil stood with his hands on his hips, belly out, and beak tup tup tupping upwards. "I think I need to stretch a bit, I'm getting a bit achy too." Boil looked up as much as his neck would allow then rolled his head from the left to the right, even managing to stretch his eye as he peered round.

Bea and Tinks joined in as it did look satisfying. They all stood with their hands on their hips and did a few squats, all poking their knobbly knees out sideways. Then they reached their arms right up as far as they would go and let them swing down in big circles. Then, for good measure, they ended with a few star jumps.

"Aaah, that's better. Now I'm ready for whatever the universe wants to throw at me," said a more centred looking Boil. Tinks was making happy chirrups and paced about a bit. It looked like she was preparing to be some sort of aeroplane, a very happy and smiley aeroplane.

"Okay Boil, shall I go first again?" offered Bea. She really did not like to keep crushing him. But before Boil had time to reply, Tinks, who was paying absolutely no attention where she was going, ran straight under where Bea was about to put her foot. Causing Bea to miss her step and spin as she fell backwards, straight down the burrow next to the portal puddle. Even though it was a Buttersquelch sized hole, Bea, in a mid–flight downwards sideways position, fit straight through. She fell backwards and head first making an echo 'Oooooooh' as she fell.

"Ooops" said Tinks as she looked up at Boil with a shrug.

"Ooops indeed!" said Boil back. "At least I know where she is. It's been a long time since I went down into the burrows. Do you have any clip lights on you?" asked Boil.

Tinks looked about herself pondering this request. Then in an 'aha' moment, with two hands poking in random directions she thrust the other two into a big pouch on the front of her jumper. She produced a small number of clip lights. Boil had no idea how they actually worked, you just had to look at them a while and they came on. Like a very bright glow instead of the beam you get from a torch. They were called clip lights because they were attached to crocodile clips. The Inklebinks were experts at making things hands free, leaving all four hands available for better use.

Boil lifted off his goggles and clipped the lights to

the spikes. He put two on one side and three on the other around his good eye. Then stretched them back and adjusted until comfy. They were small but incredibly bright lights. Every bit helped in the burrows. He could not remember much, but he remembered that it was very dark down there, the sort of dark that above ground people could never imagine.

"Tinks, I think it's best if you ride on me. If you get lost down there, I might not find you. You might fall into an even deeper burrow, one too small for me to fit through then I'd really never find you."

"Yup yup" answered Tinks as she proceeded to do what you would expect. She looked up at Boil, smiled, and stuck all of her arms in the air.

"Humpf!" Boil bent down so she could climb up his arm. Tinks swung herself up to ride piggy back on Boils neck. They did look a pair. Boil with his scruffy orange ears, his oversized eye illuminated by the clip lights on his spikey goggles, with a foot and a leg stuck out below each ear to dangle over his shoulders. His head topped with four tiny hands grabbing random bits of feather, fluff and eyebrow, and crowned with and Inklebinks grin.

"Comfy?" asked Boil rhetorically as he looked up to his shoulder.

"Yup yup" replied Tinks "Ahhaha…Hmmm"

"Must be good to be small hey" said Boil almost to himself as he turned to get into the burrow to look for Bea.

"Yup yup" muttered Tinks as she gave the top of Boils head a little nuzzle.

"Okay, let's go. Hang on tight now" Boil instructed. "Don't worry if some feathers get pulled out, they'll grow back." Tinks had no idea what he was saying and held on tight anyway.

Boil walked to the entrance of the burrow and scooched in on his bum as it was too steep to walk down. Some bits really were quite steep, going downwards and roundwards, spiralling like a floom at an aqua park.

Whumpf! Boil and Tinks landed in a crumpled heap next to Bea who was sat waiting for them.

"I knew you wouldn't be long. Glad you have lights too, it's pretty dark down here, but that's okay. I don't mind the dark." Bea looked at Boil with his face all lit up, it was a touching and welcome sight for sore eyes.

Bea was not just saying that she did not mind the dark, she actively enjoyed it! Sometimes she even preferred night times when the Moon was full and bright. She loved to gaze up at it, to look at the craters that were made by comets smashing into it millions of years ago, and to imagine flying about in the stars. It was also a lot quieter at night times, no traffic, no people rushing about racing time, everything was just calmer.

"Here, I saw this on the way down and grabbed it." Bea produced the biggest Snubgrub that Boil had ever seen.

"Aaaaww wow! Look at that! They must get fatter the darker it gets." And without a second thought Boil gobbled it up and licked his beak, all in one swift move.

"Thanks Bea."

CHAPTER ELEVEN

Bea, Boil and Tinks all looked up at the burrow they had either climbed down or fallen out of. Without anybody having to say anything they knew that they were not climbing back out again very easily. So, the trio turned and started to walk along to the next one hoping it would be a simpler climbing prospect. At least these deep tunnels were big enough for Bea to walk through comfortably. As she walked, she brushed her fingertips along the walls either side of her to make sure that she did not walk into them, she had already accumulated quite an assortment of little knocks and bumps and did not need any more. They all walked with a slow yet determined pace until they reached a significant bend.

"Boil! can you shine your light on the walls, they feel different." Bea stopped walking and looked into the shadowy wall, twiddling bits of what felt like plants in her fingers.

"Yep, here you go." Boil turned around to look at Bea looking at the wall, and pointed his head in the same direction.

"Aah, what pretty little flowers, they all look so delicate. How on earth do flowers grow all the way down here? Where do you think they came from?" asked Boil to himself again as much to anyone.

"I've no idea." said Bea gazing harder at the picture unfolding before her. "It's magical!" It was actually growing before her very eyes, translucent petals un-curling, hair thin roots investigating, spreading up and across the curve of the burrow wall. They got thicker when they got into the light from Boil. Their spindly tendrils hung on like bony fingers, excavating all the nooks and crannies. Flowers like eyes blinking at their first light. From the tendrils grew leaves and grass-es, with the greens photosynthesizing, changing into different shades, and getting brighter the longer they watched.

"It must be the light from you Boil, it's feeding it. I guess they don't have a lot of it down here, if any." observed Bea. Boil gave a 'hmmmm' in agreement and slowly moved his head in a big circle to move the light around. It was true! The flowers and leaf tips followed, reaching towards the light.

While Bea and Boil were examining the plant life born before them, Tinks had climbed off Boil and had blipped over to Beas ankle. Bea leant down to give her a hand. Tinks climbed up her arm to her shoulder and took a pew. Bea leaned her shoulder to the wall so Tinks could reach as well.

"Aaaah...alive! Awww..." said Tinks as she curi-ously moved her fingers towards a flower. This flow-er appeared to mirror Tinks and lean inwards towards her too. It reminded Bea of the way a cat will gingerly smell your hand before it lets you stroke it. This gentle touch encouraged the foliage even more as it swayed and waved, almost breathing. The colours also got more electric and intense in places where it had been touched. This must be the way a flower smiles.

Boil took a step back to get a better look. The plant life had grown exponentially since he first looked at it a few minutes ago. There was green life most of the way up the walls and it ran along the sides of the footpath, but not in the middle. It was obviously an intelligent plant and did not want to get trampled on.

"Do you want to stay up here Tinks?" asked Bea and turned back towards the bend ahead.

"Nope!" And with that Tinks swung herself round and shimmied down Beas arm and dropped to the floor. She did bounce a bit on landing but just brushed herself off and started after Boil, who had already started walking. "Nup nup nup…" She muttered to herself as she bounced along.

Bea smiled and used this quiet time to reflect a bit on her day. It dawned on her that she was in a burrow, in a world that was not her own and seeing things that she could not explain. She thought back to the Megabink with its deep soft fur, and gave the crystal that Boil had given her a rub though her pocket to comfort herself. She was looking forward to being at home, on her bed, playing with her memories and writing them all down. Her retrospective moment was then disturbed with a grumble, then again with a grumbly mumblyoooo.

"Oh belly, is that you again?" asked Bea looking down to her chatty belly as she rubbed it with both hands. "I know belly I know, I'm hungry. It might feel like we are stuck on the other side of the universe but we will be home soon." Bea gave it a last rub as it gave a final whimper of a 'mumblyooo'.

Bea lifted her head in time to see Boil peering around a bend ahead. "Wait Boil!" she shouted as she skipped to catch up.

"No problems there Bea," Boil was keeping his feet firmly planted where they were but reached his beak round as far as it would go. "I think somebody is there, listen…" Bea and Tinks joined Boil and all three stayed still, ears pricked, with senses on full alert.

There was a hussshhhing whoossshhing sound, a quiet pause and then more sounds. It was rhythmic, it was breathing! It was something that sounded asleep. The air was warmer too. Bea and Boil looked at each other, then down to Tinks. They all evaluated their environment, but Tinks did it with her eyes closed and a slightly bobbing head. Then she laughed, opened her eyes and confidently walk-jumped round the corner.

"Well, that solves that problem. Whatever it is, if it was bad then she would have stayed put or walked backwards," concluded Boil. "I'm sure I heard something else though," Boil gave the back of his ears an itch and tilted his head in thought.

"Oh," chuckled Bea. "Erm, I think that was my belly you were hearing. It wants feeding again." Said Bea grinning as she put a hand on Boils shoulder to move him round the bend. "It's okay though, I told it we would be home soon enough."

"Yes, we will eventually. Ah-ha-ha-ha," they laughed, relaxed, and returned their focus to the new lifeform that awaited them. As they regained control of their chuckles the whole burrow seemed to echo with a deep resonating rumble.

"Okay," said Bea. "Not my belly that time!"

CHAPTER TWELVE

Bea and Boil made it round the bend and saw Tinks sat next to what looked like a giant nostril. As Boil moved closer more of the strange head was lit up. Whatever it was it was definitely asleep. Warm puffs of breath were rising like steam from a hot spring. Boil looked at the walls now overgrown with all kinds of vegetation. Thick tendrils the size of arms coiled themselves like springs were wound amongst everything. Leaves and vines unfurled from the ceiling and flowers mutated from a sprinkle to an abundance of technicolour.

While Boil was looking around, Tinks had managed to climb up some roots that seemed to grow out of this beast's nose, and sat right between its eyes. Then with all four hands she proceeded to bang its head. "Knock, knock, knock, knock," said Tinks as she kept banging while swaying a bit and almost broke in to song as she shouted 'knock, knock' over and over again.

"Tinks! What on earth are you doing up there?" said Bea, a bit taken aback at just how brazen Tinks was being. "Should you really be banging its head like that, you might upset it."

"Nope, nope. Knock, KNOCK, KNOCK, KNOCK."

Tinks shouted even louder and banged even harder. Then she actually rolled over and pulled up one of its eyelids. Bea was flabbergasted!

"Tinks! Leave that poor thing alone, what are you doing to its face?" Bea was concerned, but also had to hide a laugh as the whole scene did look pretty funny. With all this commotion atop its brow the creature began to stir.

Its eyebrows arched, its nostrils wiggled and twitched, and its mouth opened and closed as it licked its lips. It repeated this process a few times in the same way that we all do when woken from a long sleep. It drew in a big breath and slowly exhaled. Tinks was still relentlessly banging caught up in her own excitement, and now singing so loudly that she had no idea that the creature beneath her had woken up. It lifted its heavy eyelid and rolled a big brown eye up to the lively little Inklebink that was clearly having a huge amount of fun.

"Hmmmmmmmm...Hellooooo," The creatures head took up almost all of the burrow and its voice sounded like you would expect, like a cave trying to talk. Low, deep, and saturated with a calm vibration. It had a long head and a wide mouth. Its eyelashes were green, grassy, and peppered with little white flowers and it did indeed, have tendrils growing out of its nose. Silk white root hairs made a map over its face and cheeks and it had large purple flowers blooming from its ears. The foliage that framed its face looked like a dense Lions mane made from plants. This attracted Tinks, as instead of crawling down and off, she moved further up its head to the space between its ears. She parted the leafy grass and nestled in to indulge in another little rest.

"Hello," said Bea in a delayed reply. "Sorry about our friend up there, she gets a bit carried away. My name is Bea, this is Boil, and that's Tinks."

"Hi there!" said Boil as he gave a greeting wave. "How long have you been down here for friend? There are plants growing all over you, in fact, I think they are growing out of you?" Boil looked and pointed to the swathes of plant life, mainly pointing to its nose.

"Aaaahh…Hmmmm, I could not say how long. Hmmmmm," He pondered this, you could almost see the thought moving through his brain. "A very long time indeed, my name is, urm…Oh. I might have to think about that a while, I have not said it in such a long time, I'm not sure I even have a name any more" he mused. "Call me…erm…" his eyes drifted about as he tried to think of something.

"I have an idea for a name. I think I'll call you Ooma. Your voice sounds like it belongs to an Ooma." said Bea thoughtfully.

"Ooooomaaa. Yes, that is good. Thank you." The corners of his lips curled upwards to a smile. "The plants are all mine, I mean, they are me. I make them. I move through these tunnels myself so slowly, but I can make these plants grow really fast. It's like somehow the bits of me that used to make me move fast got swapped with the bits of a plant that make it grow slow," Ooma took a few breaths then carried on. "Then along the way we just became the same being. They go ahead of me and explore. They are half controlled by my brain so I can direct them, unfortunately that also means that my brain is part compost." Ooma took several more pauses whilst explaining this. He must be very old to be doing everything so slowly, even by plant standards! It takes so long to say anything that he needed to make sure it was being said right. He had no arms or legs either, just moved along in little shuffles like a worm. Then Beas belly rumbled again.

"Sorry about that, almost dinnertime" said Bea blushing slightly. Not that anybody could tell down here in the dark.

"Aaah! I can help you there. All of the flowers I make are edible. Do you like flowers?" asked Ooma.

"Yes! I most certainly do," declared Boil, "I love flowers." And he began to look around with new eyes, like a kid in a sweet shop. "Do you mind?" asked Boil as he licked his beak and tapped his fingertips together.

"Oh ha-ha, go ahead please. I don't often get the pleasure of company for dinner." Ooma lolled out his huge tongue wrapping the tip around a whole bunch of flowers and whipped them into his mouth. He ate like a cow, sort of rolling his jaw sideways instead of up and down. Boil, (as I'm sure you can imagine) grabbed a couple of handfuls and shoved it into his face. Bea, being slightly more aware, picked a selection of different coloured flowers and ate them one at a time.

"Nope," said Bea. "I've not eaten flowers before, but they are delicious. I can't think what the taste reminds me of, but I love it. It's kind of fruity. I expected it to taste just like grass." Bea gobbled up her handful then put some in her pockets for dessert later on. "Thank you so much, they have really filled me up."

They were all munching happily until Ooma sneezed and sent Tinks flying off the top of his head into the ceiling, and at the same time covering Bea and Boil in snotty floral concoction of petals and leaf debris. Tinks hung on with two arms and looked down between her dangling feet, she took aim on Boils head and dropped down.

"Ooooo…Atchew! Do excuse me, I love all my flowers but they do tickle my nose. Ah-ha-huk-huk." Ooma had a low deep chuckle.

"Oompf! Thanks for the warning Tinks." Boil grumbled a bit as Tinks fidgeted and got comfy riding on Boils neck again.

"That's okay Ooma." Bea wiped patches of snot and plant matter from herself as she asked "Can you help us with something else, we are on our way to getting lost down here. I fell down a burrow back there and now we can't get back up. Do you know another way?"

"Oooooh, ummmmm, yes, I can help you. I can make my roots grow for you. I'll tell them to grow up the tunnel that you fell down, and then you can climb back up. It will be easier than finding a new burrow," explained Ooma. "I'll make sure they are strong and sturdy with lots of foot holes and bits to hang on to." Ooma took a deep breath in, closed his eyes, and hummed deeply. It looked like he was putting himself in some sort of trance. It was remarkable! All the plants seemed to be filled with new energy, they were bright and grew so fast they even made a slight buzzing sound. Thick fiberous roots made their way past Bea, Boil and Tinks round the bend to the aforementioned burrow.

"Thank you Ooma." Bea leaned forwards and rubbed the end of Ooma's nose, who opened his eyes ever so slowly in acknowledgement before closing them again to concentrate on his task.

The trio walked back down the tunnel which had been transformed into a web work jungle of vines and flowers. By the time they had reached the burrow it was filled with gnarled and twisted roots. Boil jumped up and hung on a root bit that was stuck out sideways and kicked his legs to test it.

"It all feels strong, I can see lots of foot and hand holes to hang on to. Ooma did an excellent job." Boil dropped back down and looked up at Bea. "What do you think?"

"I think it looks pretty good. I'm sure I can squeeze back up there. I'll give you a leg up then I'll follow." Bea looked up into the complicated darkness. "Can I have one of those clip lights first though please?"

"Of course, you can! Here you go." Boil unclipped two lights, one from each side of his goggles, which Bea then clipped to her own goggles.

"Excellent!" said Bea now feeling more confident. "Perfect. Come on Boil, I'll give you a bump up." Bea got down on one knee and put both hands under one of Boils feet and gave him a helpful shove onto the first bit of root.

"See you at the top Kiddo!" shouted Boil as he disappeared with Tinks still hanging tight across his neck.

"Yep, Right behind you." Bea hoisted herself up on to the roots and began to climb. It was actually a very satisfying climb. Bea had to twist around a couple of times, but she had always been an avid climber so enjoyed the challenge.

Bea emerged with a whole array of plant matter, snot, mud, flowers and fluff in her hair. She walked out on her hands until she was far enough out to drop her legs down, and then even more bits of debris fell from her. Boil and Tinks watched her scrabbling about and sniggered to themselves.

"You've got a little something in your hair there Bea, Ah-ha-ha-ha!" They all laughed together and shook themselves off, sending little bits of everything all over the place. "Okay, not much time I'm afraid, let's do what we planned to do before that delightful interlude" stated Boil. "Hang on Tinks," but before Tinks could realize what was actually going on Boil had lept into the air, pulled his arms and legs in tight and bulleted through the portal puddle.

"Boil hang on, wait!" shouted a slightly anxious Bea. "Oh well, here goes nothing" and followed Boil into the next dimension.

CHAPTER THIRTEEN

Bea flew out of something and landed in a crumpled heap next to Boil, who in anticipation had already rolled out of the way.

"Eeeeww, this is really dirty. What even is this?" Boil held up a wad of something that was almost fluorescent pink that was sticky and squidgy and was covered in all kinds of hair. "It's sticking to my fur and I can't get it off!" Boil tried to unstick it with one finger which also got stuck to it. "Whatever this place is, don't touch the pink stuff." Boil was getting himself in to even more of a pickle and as much as he did not mind siting on dirty floors, even he found this one pretty disgusting.

It only took Bea a moment to realize where she was, she was under the seat of a bus! No wonder the floor was so dirty. She slid herself out further and pulled out Tinks and Boil. They must have been spat out on to the seat then bounced on to the floor. It was lucky for them it was the back of a fairly empty bus.

"We're on a bus Boil, that means I'm home." Bea slapped the back shoulder of Boil in jubilation which almost knocked him over. "Here Tinks, I'll help you."

Bea lifted Tinks onto the seat then sat down herself and Boil jumped up between them.

"Okay, it's a good job we landed at the back, the driver might not see us. I don't have any money to pay him so keep your heads down," said Bea as reality was slowly sinking in.

"What is it with your world and portals in furniture?" Boil joked, making his face all wonky.

"I can't believe it, it feels strange," Bea had to acclimatize again. She was used to feeling odd, but this was something bigger, something new. As much as it was her world, where she lived, where she was real, she felt very far away.

The bus engine stopped and started and chugged along. Only a couple of people got on or off either reading books or listening to headphones, distracting themselves from bus life. So much so that nobody noticed the girl, the Buttersquelch and the Inklebink, all covered in every kind of mess, looking dreamily out of the window like everything was completely normal. Except for Tinks, who was too small to see out of the window, she just sat smiling and nodding trying not to fall off.

The bus went over bumps and potholes bouncing everyone about. Lights trailed past and the engine vibrated so much that Tinks had to keep shuffling back on her seat. Then the bus driver made an announcement for the next stop.

"Oh, hey Boil, I know where we are! We can get off here and walk to my house. Okay everyone, try to look normal." Bea stood up and helped Boil down with one hand, and then Boil helped Tinks with his other.

Bea and Boil both struck a pose (all totally normally of course) with their shoulders down and relaxed, chins up, and chests out they strutted down the isle of the bus with exaggerated swagger, hands swinging at either side. They each had their goggles on top of their heads and had big muddy rings around their eyes. Tinks was a bit overwhelmed by all the noise and mechanical vibrations so she wrapped herself around Beas leg and hung on tight.

As they walked in big strides down the bus they went past one couple who were more interested in each other than what was going on right next to them. There was a young woman who with headphones and a laptop, and on the other side there was a very large man reading an even larger newspaper.

Right at the front there were the only two people who were actually looking about. Well, one was looking about anyway. They were an elderly couple. The man was sat next to the window with one half of his face resting on it making a steam patch on the glass, the other half of his face was buried in the top of his coat and scarf. The woman however was looking all around. The lights through the window made pretty patterns reflect in her glasses as she moved. She chatted away to herself, nodding and humming and occasionally patting the knee of her other half, almost like a giant Inklebink, but with two less arms.

"Ere, Frank, look at that!" the lady with the faded

blue hair and extravagantly oversized purple fluffy cardigan said as she smacked the arm of the gentleman she was sat with.

"What Doris, what's the matter love?" The old man stirred in his coat and rolled his head to Doris. This was a sharp thwack rather than a gentle pat so she must really want his attention. He was wearing a very old coat with frayed elbow pads, and when he moved his head you could see all the grey hair growing out of his ears and lumpy nose, and all kinds sprouting from his eyebrows.

"Look at those kids, poor things. They're obviously covered in everything, what a sight!" Doris stared at the trio (though only noticing Bea and Boil) as they walked past their seat and almost got to the door. It was then that Doris got a better look at Boil. "Oh, what a strange looking child that is!" Doris pulled her hand up to her face in surprise. "Frank! Frank!"

Frank had of course rolled is chin back into the top of his coat and was happily snoozing away. Doris was trying to make sense of what she was looking at, but you could tell by the expression on her face that she was finding it difficult. As they hopped off the bus Boil turned to look at the utterly perplexed woman. He caught sight of himself in the reflection of her glasses and even he had to admit that to an untrained eye he did look a tad peculiar.

"I am not an odd child, I am a Buttersquelch!" Boil exclaimed with one finger in the air. Then with full pride he puffed his chest out as far as it would go and walked after Bea.

"A Buttersquelch Frank, what do you suppose that is?" Frank was almost snoring again but mustered enough energy for one last observation. "I've no idea dear. It must be a new thing the kids are into," he mumbled in reply.

"Yes, I suppose it must be." Doris agreed with her husband but knew he was wrong. She had witnessed something new, something special and otherworldly, something that made the child inside her smile. "Buttersquelch," she said to herself quietly, "I like that."

The bus pulled away and Bea, Boil, and a calmer Tinks set off in the other direction.

"I know exactly where I am, we're close to my house now. This path leads to the common." Bea took a right down an alley that went between two houses that led to the common with the big Cedar tree.

It's strange how things seem to move faster when you are somewhere familiar. The time seemed to move in patchy flashes like in a dream. In the blink of an eye they had travelled from the bus stop, past the Cedar tree, to the entrance to the woodland path.

"Aaaah, the woodland! The path to your garden shed and then to home." Boil looked up at Bea who was now looking pretty exhausted. Tinks also looked up and made a few happy chirrups, but stayed firmly attached to Beas leg.

"Yeah, we finally made it hey Boil" Bea said affectionately. "Come on then, dusk is almost over and it will be dark soon." Bea took Boils hand as they entered the woodland. "I wonder if it's night time in your world?"

"Oh, it will be afternoon tomorrow by now I imagine. Who knows! It's very difficult to keep track. Two Suns there, one Moon here, it's easy to get mixed up. At least it's not raining anymore." Bea and Boil shared a laugh, Tinks smiled and they all set off.

Again, as if some time had gone missing, they had arrived at the bottom of the garden. "Come in." Bea opened the rickety gate that led to the battered shed and they all went inside.

It was refreshing to smell the rust and oil, to see the screws and nuts all over the place and spiders at home in their webs. It was especially amazing to see Grandads old armchair, in all its glory, taking pride of place in the middle. Tinks dropped of Beas leg and pop-corned over to it. The chair clearly gave off good vibrations as Tinks looked almost as happy as she did banging Ooma's massive head. She rubbed a cheek on the chair which left a big smudge of well-loved dirt. Now she too looked like one of the shed people, the shed people with a population of three.

"Bea, I'll take a little nap first but then it's time for me to go back. Tinks will be fine entertaining herself for a little while." Boil wiped his arm across his head and tried not to look as weary as he felt. He sighed, relaxed his ears and exchanged a tired lopsided smile with Bea. Their faces said it all, the mutual feelings of tiredness, of joy, and of a calm happiness.

"Okay Boil, you can sleep on the chair, I know you love it. Just don't roll back until you're ready to go home," chuckled Bea. "I need to go inside now too, you've worn me out. When will I see you again? You will be back won't you?" Bea couldn't help but be tinged with a bit of sadness that her day had now come to an end and she had to part from her new friends.

"Of course!" said Boil with a big wide smile and open arms. "You just try and keep me away when I have so much more to show you! You won't get any warning though, I'll just turn up." Boil jumped onto the chair and propped himself up with one elbow on the arm rest to hold his heavy head. "You can always look at the little treasure I gave you to remind you of me," said Boil as he pointed to Beas pocket.

"Sure will." Bea reached in her secret pocket and pulled out the precious crystal on the grubby string and gave it a rub. "Thanks Boil. I'm going to add it to a necklace and wear it all the time. You keep those goggles too, they suit you and they will remind you of me." Bea leant down and gave Boil a little kiss on his eyebrow and scratched under his beak. Then went to Tinks and held her face close enough so Tinks could reach her arms up and give Beas nose a nuzzle.

"I'll miss you guys." Bea waved goodbye as Boil and Tinks got comfy and she closed the shed door.

Bea had a deep breath in and out. She looked up at the Moon that was now fully out to play and shining brightly. She closed her eyes and took one more breath, then walked up the garden path, and with one last look over her shoulder, she went inside.

THE NEXT DAY

The next morning Bea came running down the garden path, pulled open the shed door and jumped inside. There was the armchair, the screws, the lawnmower parts and a collection of rags, but no Boil or Tinks.

She walked over to the chair and rubbed her hands on it. She even shoved her head down the back of it as far as it would go but alas, she was not sucked in. It just left her standing there with bits of chair debris stuck all over her face.

She felt her heart sink a little bit then looked over to the desk. Next to the biggest greasiest bit of lawnmower engine and the radio in a million bits, there sat a peculiar set of goggles and a note...

HI BEA,

WE MADE THESE FOR YOU,
WE HOPE YOU LIKE THEM.

WE WILL SEE YOU SOON.
    IF YOU NEED ME,
SHOUT INTO THE CHAIR AND
I MIGHT HEAR YOU.
WE ARE WORLDS AWAY.
BUT IT'S NOT THAT FAR...
TAKE CARE OF YOUR BELLY
AND YOUR HEAD.

YOUR FRIENDS
    BOIL AND TINKS!

GLOSSARY OF TERMS

- Intriguing – To arouse the curiosity of; To make interesting; Compelling; Fascinating; Interesting
- Ginormous – Very large; Colossal; Huge
- Bizarre – Odd or unusual; Abnormal; Fantastic
- Conviction – A firmly held belief or opinion
- Realisation – To become aware of something
- Conclusion – Outcome of a result; a final decision of judgement
- Glorious- Brilliantly beautiful
- Curious – Eager to learn; Interesting because of oddness or novelty
- Eccentric – Irregular or odd; A person who deviates from normal behaviour
- Proclaimed – To announce publicly; To shout aloud
- Quizzically – Questioning and mocking
- Extraordinary – Unusual or surprising; Beyond what is usual
- Triumphant – The feeling of happiness from victory
- Acquaintance – A person whom one knows but is not a close friend; To come into social contact with
- Undulating – Any wave or wavelike form
- Morphing – 'Combining form' ; Indicating shape, form, or structure of any kind

- Transforming – To convert one form of energy to another
- Meandered – To follow a winding course; To wander without definite aim or direction
- Escalated – To increase or to be increased
- Conjunction – The act of joining together
- Indulge – To allow the pleasure of something
- Extravagant – Going beyond the usual bounds
- Dramatic – Acting or performed in a flamboyant way; Striking or effective
- Focusing – The state of an optical image when it is distinct and clearly defined
- Hibernated – To cease from activity; To pass the winter in a dormant condition with metabolism greatly slowed down
- Fraction – A small piece; Fragment
- Portal – An entrance, gateway or doorway
- Genuine – Original; Real; Authentic
- Deflated – To take away the self esteem
- Acclimatize – To adapt or become accustomed to a new climate or environment
- Aroma – A distinctive usually pleasant smell
- Furrowing – (Furrow) – Any long deep groove, especially a deep wrinkle on the forehead
- Assertive – Given to making assertions; Dogmatic
- Propelled – To cause to move forwards
- Dimension – A new aspect of something
- Gestured – A motion of the hands, head or body to express an idea or emotion
- Particular – Especially or exactly

- Expression – A manifestation of an emotion or feeling
- Humorous – Funny; Comical; Amusing
- Dismantle – To take apart
- Delicate – Precise or delicate in action
- Accumulated – To become gathered together in increasing quantity
- Diffracted – A deviation in the direction of a wave at the edge of an obstacle in its path. (a light wave hitting the crystal and bouncing off it in a different direction)
- Amethyst – A purple or Violet variety of quartz used as a gem stone
- Flummoxed – To perplex or bewilder
- Logical – Characterized by clear or valid reasoning
- Gibberish – Rapid chatter; Incomprehensible talk
- Insightful – The ability to understand one's own problems
- Dexterity – Physical skill or nimbleness
- Kerfuffle – Commotion; Disorder
- Proportion – Correct relationship between parts
- Frantically – Showing frenzy
- Reciprocated – To give or feel in return
- Vibrations – Instinctive feelings supposedly influencing human communication
- Summoned – Ordered to come
- Docile – Easy to manage
- Temperament – The characteristic way an individual behaves
- Inquisitive – Eager to learn; Excessively curious
- Immense – Massive; Huge; Vast
- Blissful – Serenely joyful or glad

- Mantra – Speech used as an instrument of thought
- Apprehensive – Fearful or anxious
- Cascaded – Something resembling a waterfall
- Haunches – The fleshy hindquarters of an animal
- Monumental – Like a monument, especially large in size
- Shimmied – To vibrate or wobble
- Delectable – Highly enjoyable
- Reminisced – To talk or write about past experiences
- Captivated – To hold the attention by fascinating or enchanting
- Static electric – Electric sparks or crackling produced by friction
- Contemplated – To think about intently or at length
- Saturated – To fill, soak or imbue totally
- Cacophony – Harsh discordant sound
- Abdomen – The posterior part of the body behind the thorax
- Camouflaged – The means by which an animal escapes the notice of predators
- Unfurling – To unroll, unfold or spread out
- Spores – A germ cell, seed, dormant bacterium; Produced by many plants
- Vigorous – Applying bodily or mental strength or vitality
- Exponentially – Very rapidly
- Prescribed – To lay down as a rule or directive
- Pondering – To give thorough or deep fascination
- Rhetorically – A question to which no answer is needed
- Translucent – Allowing light to pass through

- Excavating – To make a hole or tunnel in solid matter by hollowing
- Photosynthesizing – The transformation (synthesizing) of organic compounds from carbon dioxide and water using light energy absorbed by chlorophyll (the green pigment in plants)
- Retrospective – Looking backwards in time
- Resonating – To resound or reverberate
- Abundance – A copious supply; A great amount
- Technicolour – (Trademark) A process of producing colour film
- Brazen – Shameless and bold
- Flabbergasted – To be utterly amazed
- Commotion – Confused noise; Din
- Relentlessly – Sustained; Unremitting
- Concoction – To make by combining different ingredients
- Aforementioned – Stated or mentioned before
- Anticipation – The act of expectation
- Jubilation – The act of rejoicing
- Exaggerated – To make greater; More noticeable
- Perplexed – To puzzle, bewilder or confuse
- Peculiar – Strange or unusual
- Otherworldly – Relating to the imaginative world

Index

Bea and the Buttersquelch